This book belongs to

_____

With special thanks to Alan Stewart, Professor of Ecology at the University of Sussex and convenor of the Royal Entomological Society's Insect Conservation Special Interest Group, for reviewing the text and pictures – D.C.

For Sungah, Luah and my dear parents – S.L.

The artwork in this book was handcrafted using watercolour and coloured pencils and finished with digital methods.

Printed on sustainably sourced FSC® certified paper. Uses plant-based inks which reduce chemical emissions.

First published in 2024 by Floris Books. This paperback edition published in 2024
Text © 2024 Dawn Casey. Illustrations © 2024 Stella Lim (스텔라 임). Dawn Casey and Stella Lim have asserted their right under the Copyright, Designs and Patent Act 1988 to be identified as the Author and Illustrator of this Work. All rights reserved.
No part of this book may be reproduced without the prior permission of Floris Books, Edinburgh www.florisbooks.co.uk British Library CIP data available
ISBN 978-178250-903-5 Printed in China by Leo Paper Products Ltd

FSC
www.fsc.org
MIX
Paper | Supporting
responsible forestry
FSC® C020056

The Bumblebee Garden

Dawn Casey and Stella Lim

Floris Books

It was the very beginning of spring. Ben and Grandpa were busy in the garden.

"Look, Grandpa!" Ben pointed. A fat fuzzy bumblebee.

ziggety-zag, ziggety-zag

buzzz-ump

The bee peeked into a little hole in the earth.

"Ah," said Grandpa. "A queen bee, looking for somewhere to nest."

The wind blew. Snowdrops shivered. "Isn't she cold?" asked Ben.

Grandpa smiled. "Her thick coat keeps her warm."

Ben buttoned up his warm coat. "Me too!"

Outside, rain was falling.

*pitter-patter,
splash-splish*

Inside, Ben was playing, softening beeswax in his hands. He squeezed it and shaped it. He rolled it into a good long worm.

"Grandpa," said Ben, "where do bumblebees go when it rains?"

"Well, by now the queen will have found a little hole in the ground. She'll be warm and dry inside her nest today."

"Just like us!" said Ben.

"Just like us," said Grandpa. "She keeps her food in a little wax pot, so that even on rainy days, when it's too wet to fly, she has plenty to eat."

Ben coiled his wax round and round. "There," he said, "I've made a pot too."

One day, Grandpa and Ben had a picnic in the garden, with Ben's baby sister, Hana Mae.

Ben watched the queen bee fly out of her nest under the hedge.
She flew over to the daisies and back again. "What's she doing, Grandpa?"

"Well," said Grandpa, "inside her nest, the queen laid her eggs.
Out of each egg came a little larva – small and plump and wiggly."

"Like Hana Mae!" said Ben.

Grandpa laughed. "Yes, a little like Hana Mae. The queen is collecting pollen from the flowers, to feed her larvae..."

Ben nodded. He passed Hana Mae the dish, full of good things to eat.

num, num, nummm

"Sometime soon," said Grandpa, "when the larvae have grown big and strong, each one will do something very special."

"What, Grandpa?"

"Each little larva will spin itself a silk cocoon."

Ben found a blanket. He took one end and gave the other end to Hana Mae. She held on tight. "Now spin!" said Ben.

wheee...

Hana Mae spun round and round. The blanket wound around her until, *plump*, she sat down, laughing.

"Look Grandpa," said Ben, "Hana Mae is a cocoon!"

By summertime, there were lots of busy bees.

"Where have they all come from?" said Ben.

"From the cocoons, of course," said Grandpa. "Inside their cocoons, each little larva turned into a bee!"

The bees feasted on the flowers, sipping the sweet nectar.

zip-zip, sip-sip

On one white blossom, a bumblebee hummed.

"Look Grandpa," said Ben. "On her back legs. Little yellow balls..."

"Ah, you've spotted the bee's pockets," said Grandpa. "She fills them with pollen to feed her baby sisters in the nest."

"I know!" said Ben. "Let's give our berries to *my* baby sister!"

The strawberries were sweet and juicy. Hana Mae was very happy.

squeeze... squash... slip... slurp

"You know," said Grandpa, "we only have these berries because of the bees."

"What do you mean?" asked Ben.

"Well, when bees visit flowers, they carry pollen from one flower to another. The pollen helps turn the flowers into fruits."

Ben took a bite of his strawberry. *Mmmm.* "Thank you, bees..."

Ben was quiet for a while, thinking. "Grandpa... the bees feed me, so... could we feed the bees?"

Grandpa grinned. He nodded his head. "Yes," he said. "We can."

At summer's end, Grandpa and Ben worked side by side. They cleared the ground. They dug and they raked.

Grandpa held out a rustly paper bag. "Wildflower seeds," he said.

"In winter they'll dream. In spring they'll grow. And in summer they'll flower, and give their nectar and pollen to the bees."

Ben sprinkled the seeds onto the soil. Very gently, he covered them over with a fine blanket of earth.

pat-pat

"Night, night. Sweet dreams."

In the autumn, Ben and Grandpa tidied up the garden.

scrunch-crunch

"Not too neat," said Grandpa. "The queen bees will need somewhere safe to sleep through the winter."

So Grandpa and Ben left one part of the garden wild. They let the weeds be, they let the grass grow. They didn't rake up the fallen leaves or cut back the ivy. And in a shady spot, Ben made a pile of old logs. "A bedroom fit for a queen!"

Winter came. By suppertime the sun had set, and by bedtime the stars were bright.

Grandpa looked out at the garden. "All the bumblebee queens are fast asleep now," he said, "hibernating 'til the spring."

zzzzz...

Ben snuggled into his blanket. "I like hibernating too."

Day by day, the year turned. Winter became
spring. In the earth, the seeds woke up.
So did the queen bees.

The wildflowers put down roots and sent up shoots. The queen bees found nests and laid eggs.

Fat buds swelled.
So did wiggly larvae.

By summertime, the garden was bright with flowers,
a feast for the bumblebees.

bzzzzzzzzzz...........

The Life Cycle of a Queen Bumblebee

1 At the very beginning of spring, the queen wakes up and looks for somewhere to nest.

2 She finds a little hole to nest in. Perhaps an old mouse hole, soft with moss.

3 In her nest, she makes a wax pot. She gathers nectar from the flowers to fill it with food.

9 Each queen bee finds somewhere safe and warm to hibernate through the winter.

8 Some female bees are helpers, others grow into queens. Each queen finds a mate, a male from a different nest.

4 The queen lays her eggs inside the nest and keeps them warm.

5 Little larvae hatch out. The queen gathers pollen from flowers for them to eat.

6 When they have eaten enough, each larva spins a cocoon.

7 Out of each cocoon comes a bee! Some are male, others are female.